THE
COLLABORATIVE
WAY

*A Story About
Engaging the
Mind and Spirit
of a Company*

Lloyd Fickett and Jason Fickett

LF&A PUBLISHING

Published by: LF&A Publishing
83 Vaquero Drive
Boulder, CO 80303
303-499-0766

Find us on the World Wide Web at: www.collaborativeway.com

Book Design by Kathryn Jenkins
Printed and bound in the U.S.A.

Library of Congress Cataloging-in-Publication Data

Fickett, Lloyd.
  The collaborative way : a story about engaging the mind and spirit of a company / Lloyd Fickett and Jason Fickett.
    p. cm.
    LCCN 2006910680
    ISBN-13: 978-0-9788963-1-7
    ISBN-10: 0-9788963-1-9

    1. Leadership—Fiction. 2. Teams in the workplace—Management—Fiction. 3. Organizational effectiveness—Fiction. I. Fickett, Jason. II. Title.

    PS3606.I29C65 2007   813'.6
                                QBI06-600708

In Appreciation

of the courage, heart and leadership of all of those who step forward each day and practice The Collaborative Way.

TABLE OF CONTENTS

THE
PROLOGUE

A little over three years ago…

I called my wife and told her not to wait for me to eat. I said, "I need the best food on Earth tonight."

"Are you in the car?" she asked. "Barry Halton, you're not driving to Phoenix right now, are you?"

Helen knew me too well. I said I needed the best food and the best wine. "I just called Lincoln Ranch Grill on my cell. I've got reservations at the restaurant, and there's room at the hotel there, too. I've got that early morning meeting up in Phoenix tomorrow. It's all working out!"

"What's going on, Barry? What's wrong?"

She saw right through my momentary excitement. I was an open book to her. I said, "It feels like we're stuck headed down the same path as my first company. It's only been four years since I started this company, and we're already caught in the same bad habits as the first one. We're not working together as a team. Our financial reports all look good, but I know better. And it's just a matter of time until the competition heats up. When it does, we're going to be in trouble."

❖

Whenever I've been down, I've always remembered the advice the famous psychologist Carl Jung gave to a depressed woman: He told her to eat well. I drove the hundred miles to my favorite restaurant and ordered my favorite dish—a delicious roasted duck—and a bottle of wine. My plan was to savor the meal, have a couple glasses and figure things out.

Just like with my first company, Halton Homes, we'd had a great start-up. Sonoran Communities grew quickly, and soon we were so big I couldn't directly manage all the people who were running our projects. Then—just like at Halton Homes—some of the projects started not making budget, and the project teams started selfishly fighting over resources. We were still coming out ahead. In fact, the last year had been our best ever financially. But the bickering among business units and the turf warfare were going to kill us as soon as the playing field heated up. I knew the competition was going to get tougher, and we needed to be ready. I'd tried a lot of different things, but nothing yet had helped us become the team we needed to be.

❖

I was in the middle of enjoying my delicious meal when I saw him being seated. He and his wife were with another couple. I dabbed my face with my napkin and tried to look away, but there was nowhere to go. He saw me. He hesitated and squinted, then smiled and started to come over.

"Barry Halton!"

It was John Caffey, my old vice-president at Halton Homes. He was about the last person I wanted to see.

"Hey, Caffey." I smiled weakly. He'd been with me from the very beginning, when we'd started with a vision for reinventing tract-home communities and taken the Phoenix suburbs by surprise. He'd stuck with me through all our struggles and then, regrettably, lost his job not long after I sold to the big national, Rycor Communities. I still felt bad about it. I wouldn't have thought he would be so happy to see me. I stood up and we shook hands.

"How long has it been? How are you doing?" He was excited. He clapped me on the arm.

"It's got to be more than five years," I said.

"You look good. How are you doing?"

"Good. Just trying to eat and drink well." I held up my glass of wine. "Doctor's orders." I took another sip. "I didn't know you knew this place."

"We just started coming here this past year. We brought some friends," he nodded over to his table. I waved to his wife.

I asked him if he'd ever tried the wine I was drinking, and we both sat down. I showed him the bottle. "It's a Pinot. You should try some. I'll order you a bottle. You can't get it anywhere else. I'm still on a waiting list from the vineyard." I waved my waiter over and ordered a bottle for Caffey's table.

Caffey thanked me. "This is great, running into you. I'd just recently decided I wanted to call you, and then I run into you here. It's funny how life works sometimes."

I was surprised he was happy to see me. I'd thought about getting in touch with him a number of times, too, but I always kind of dreaded it. I felt like I'd hung him out to dry, without meaning to, when I sold Halton Homes. "I was glad to hear you landed on your feet after Halton," I said. "I heard you got on at Pinnacle Homes. Congratulations."

"Thanks. Things are really going well for me there. It's such a different kind of company to work for. It took some getting used to, but I love it now."

I wasn't sure why, but I felt defensive. "What's so different about it?"

"Our commitment to collaboration. It runs throughout

the company. At first, I resisted changing from being the kind of leader I thought I was supposed to be. But since taking on this different way of working together, I've become a much better leader. I've even grown personally from it."

I was intrigued. "That sounds interesting."

"Listen, Barry." Caffey leaned forward. "The reason I'd wanted to call you is to thank you for the important contribution you made to my life. I can't thank you enough for giving me my start in this business. Without the opportunity you gave me to be a vice-president at Halton Homes, I'm not sure what I'd be doing now. You saw something in me long before I did, and you've contributed a great deal to me."

I was stunned. "Wow. Thanks for saying that." The last thing I expected from Caffey was an acknowledgement.

He said, "I mean it. I can see now what an enormous contribution you made to me."

I didn't know what to say. I moved my wine glass in a small circle on the table.

Caffey said, "And I heard you've got a new company! You're down in Tucson, right? What's the name of your company?"

"Sonoran Communities," I told him. "I couldn't name this one after myself."

"That's great." He looked back at his wife and friends. "I really should get back. But I'd love to catch up some more. If you're interested, I'd like to share some more about the collaborative approach we've taken on at Pinnacle, too. I think it could have made a big difference back at Halton. Why don't you come over to my house for lunch this weekend and we could talk?"

I was a little suspicious about how much Caffey wanted to share this 'collaborative approach' with me. I felt resistant to it; I wasn't sure why. But I did want to catch up with him. He had been a good friend of mine. "Sure," I said. "It's been a long time. I'd love to come over." We made plans to meet at his house that Saturday.

We stood up and shook hands again, and Caffey said, "I'm really glad we ran into each other. Thanks again for the wine."

I ate the rest of my dinner awed by our brief exchange. I was a little surprised I had agreed to go over to Caffey's house so quickly, and I was still shocked by his thanks. Helen would enjoy hearing about this. She'd always thought it was a shame Caffey and I had lost touch.

❖

Caffey's house was in north Phoenix, set against the desert preserve. His front yard was thick with creosote bushes and old palo verde trees. Two red, shorthaired dogs, happy and barking, ran out to the car to greet me as I parked.

Caffey was in the middle of making lunch for us. His wife and two kids had gone out to the mall and to a movie. "I wanted us to have some peace and quiet so we could talk. Shopping and a movie wasn't a hard sell."

We had homemade chicken burritos. "I never get tired of this meal," Caffey said. "Just take some chicken from one of those store-cooked ones, heat it up with some cheese on a tortilla in the toaster oven, add some shredded cabbage and carrots, a little cottage cheese, some salsa and a few slices of avocado. Delicious!"

We caught up over lunch. I told him about our move to Tucson, about the town and our new house. He told me about his kids and the vacation he and his wife took to Fiji.

We cleared the table together and went into the living

room. I sat down in a wide, cushioned wicker-back chair. Caffey took the gray leather couch. The dogs followed him up and got comfortable, one on each side.

Caffey chuckled. "I don't know how it's come to this, but we're letting these mutts up on this thing now." He petted their heads. "How'd you mutts manage to pull it off?"

"I forgot what kind of dogs those are. They're beautiful animals," I said.

"They're Vizslas. They're Hungarian bird dogs."

"That's right." I nodded. "I see Diane finally talked you into getting another one."

"That was a couple years ago. You're out of the loop. Now she's pushing for number three. She's getting into training them. You should see our backyard. We have a huge dog agility course out there."

"Two kids and three dogs? That's a crowded house."

"Once she gets this passionate about something, it's inevitable." One of the dogs rolled over, and he petted her belly.

"You know, Caffey," I said hesitantly, "I was really surprised to hear the acknowledgment you gave me when we met the other night. When I heard you lost your job, I felt terrible about it. I thought for sure you were going to be angry with me."

Caffey said, "I have to admit I was angry at you at first. But I've come to recognize that you weren't the only one responsible for what happened at Halton. I played a big role, too. In many ways I let you and everyone else at Halton down. I also recognize that by selling Halton when you did, you kept all the crews at work. You saved their jobs. I know how committed you've always been to your workforce."

I didn't know what to say. I didn't think anyone would ever appreciate that saving people's jobs was one of my motivations for selling Halton to Rycor. "Thanks for saying that. That means a lot to me."

"I thought it might. I had a feeling nobody had ever really acknowledged you for that. And I'm sure you've got that same commitment to your workforce at your new company."

"It's one of my core values." I was proud of that.

"So, Barry, how's it going at your new company?"

I let my eyes wander the room before I answered. "If I'd run into you a year or two ago, I could have held my head high and told you things were great. You know, just like last time, the start-up was great—in some ways, even better than it was at Halton. And according to the numbers, we just came off our best year yet. But it feels just like before, like those last few years at Halton. Too often, I'm finding it necessary to take over sites because they're not making budget. The sense of team we had during the first two years is already degenerating into infighting. I feel like all it would take now is for another Rycor to come into town and we'd end up in real danger. I thought I'd figured out everything that went wrong at Halton before I started Sonoran." I shook my head. "To be honest, I'm starting to think I'm not cut out to lead a company past the start-up. I should just sell now and start another one. Or maybe find something completely different to do. Maybe it's a sign, though, that I ran into you."

I hadn't looked at Caffey the whole time I was talking. I felt like I had just unburdened myself. When I looked up, he was still petting his dogs.

"Sorry to dump my troubles on you, but you asked."

Caffey reassured me, "No, that's fine. I appreciate you being honest with me. I had a hunch that might be the case when I saw you at the restaurant. Maybe it's a part of why I invited you over. You brought me into this business and gave me a great opportunity, Barry. If I can help you now, I'd really like to. I've learned some things in the past few years at Pinnacle that I think could provide a pathway for you to get through the barrier you seem to have run up against in your new company."

"I appreciate you wanting to help." I was grateful he was trying to help me, but I was still resistant to any 'pathway' he was going to provide me. "You seem really excited about working at Pinnacle."

"I am; it's a great place to work. I feel fulfilled, contributing everything I can. It's a testament to what our CEO, Roy Messer, has built."

"I've heard Roy is a great leader."

"Roy's amazing. But he's not alone at Pinnacle. There are a lot of great leaders there. And my leadership ability has grown tremendously as a result of working there. Roy sees building leaders as being as much a part of his job as building homes. He hasn't done it all by himself, though. A big part of his approach is something we call The Collaborative Way."

I couldn't help making a face. "The Collaborative Way? Sounds kind of touchy-feely. What is it?"

Caffey laughed. "Touch-feely? No, it's more like a tool set. That's what Roy calls it. It's a set of tools for working together effectively. It also provides tools for being a leader. It's a way people can work together to get the results they want. Working there feels like it did back in the old days when we first started Halton."

"I miss that." Even though I'd had that same feeling again when I started Sonoran, I felt discouraged now. I wondered why I hadn't been able to keep that energy alive.

"Maybe it will be easier to explain if I draw you a quick

picture. Let me get some paper and a pen."

"You can use this." I handed him a note pad and pen from my shirt pocket.

Caffey said, "You still carry a pad and pen all the time?"

"I'd be lost without it. It keeps me out of a lot of trouble, provided I read what I have written down. Otherwise, I forget almost everything."

As Caffey drew a circle sketch on the paper, I sat back in my chair and crossed my arms and legs. I started to wonder what I had gotten myself into. It was great being with Caffey again, but now I was feeling a little uncomfortable about where we were headed. I hoped this wasn't going to turn into some kind of sermon.

"Here's the basic design," Caffey said as he tore out the page he had been working on and looked up at me. He hesitated as he started to hand me the page. "Are you sure you want me to explain this to you? I can't tell, but you seem bothered or something."

I laughed. "Yeah, I'd like to hear more. I guess I just have a hard time believing it will be something that I can really use. But please go on."

"Some of it might challenge the way you think about things."

"I'm always interested in learning something new." That's what I said, but I had a feeling it was going to be another one of those new management techniques. I'd already heard plenty of those.

"OK. You said you thought you'd figured out everything that went wrong with Halton before you started your new company. What were some of the mistakes you believe you made?"

That was an easy one for me to answer. "First, I hired

and promoted the wrong people. They didn't have the brains and spirit I thought they did. I needed people who were up for change, who were ready to change so we could stay competitive. And then, I let things go too long. I didn't intervene soon enough. I didn't make personnel changes quickly enough. That meant I had to come up with too many of the solutions myself, and when we got too big that just didn't work anymore."

"Have you had any of those same problems with Sonoran? Any of those same feelings about the people you hired?"

"Yeah, but I've started to realize that people never cease to disappoint me."

Caffey nodded knowingly. "What if there's something about the way you're leading that's contributing to why things are turning out the same way again?"

"Like I already said, I'm starting to wonder if there is something wrong with my leadership. Maybe I'm not cut out for taking a company beyond this point."

"You're too hard on yourself, Barry. I think in many ways you're already a great leader. You have one of the highest standards of integrity I've ever run into, and you are always learning. You call Halton a failure, but most people would love to have that kind of success. You built that company up from nothing into one of the most successful construction companies in Phoenix and sold while it was at the height of its success. That's pretty damn good, if you ask me. At Pinnacle, we're just now taking on some of the initiatives you were trying to make happen at the end at Halton. You have great vision and you're a great strategist. I just think you have a couple blind spots that keep you from being able to bring it all together. I think if you were more collaborative in the way you lead, you could get past this limit you seem to have reached again. It's nothing beyond what you're capable of learning. It might take a lot of hard work, but you're good at that. And if I can learn it, you sure can."

We both laughed.

"OK, Caffey, thanks for the pep talk. I think I needed that. Now would you let me see your diagram?"

Caffey leaned forward and handed me the drawing. "OK, but if you don't find this useful as we move forward, please let me know. I value our time together too much to want to waste it."

Caffey moved over to the matching cushioned chair beside me, and we looked at the diagram together.

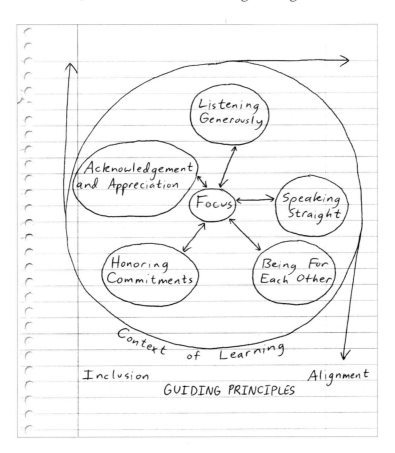

"So, at the center of it there's 'Focus.' This is the part where you define your goals and your company vision. And these five commitments," he pointed to the five circles surrounding the center, "support you in getting what you want. The five commitments are basically ways of working and relating together that give you the most power.

"Under here you have the guiding principles, 'Inclusion' and 'Alignment.' They're about keeping the collaboration going. This kind of cradle part," he pointed again, "is 'Context of Learning,' which is a guide for how you practice The Collaborative Way."

"What do you mean, 'A guide for how you practice'?"

"Well, people often turn a design like this into a way to make other people wrong for what they're doing or as another way to beat themselves up. Context of Learning means realizing no one will ever master this way of working together. The whole point is to keep learning and improving. One way to do that is to be open to other people's support. It's like the saying 'It's the journey, not the destination.'"

"Did Roy make all this up?"

"No, no." Caffey leaned back in his chair and crossed his legs. "We've just been practicing it for about ten years, so it's really ingrained in our culture."

I pointed at the drawing and asked, "What are those arrows?"

"Those are the outcomes of working this way: teamwork, organizational speed and agility and a satisfying work environment. And like I said, all of it's centered on your company's focus and organizational direction. It's there to serve what you want to accomplish with your company, whatever your vision is."

I said. "We recently refined our vision. Now it's: 'We will build a great company that's one of the top three homebuilders in our market and that provides leadership in the industry by building medium-priced homes with a high-quality aesthetic, high energy efficiency and environmental sensitivity.'"

"That sounds great. I'm not surprised you're up to providing leadership for the industry while also building a great company. I would expect you to be doing something visionary. That's what The Collaborative Way would be centered on, you reaching that goal."

That sounded good but I was curious about something. "This might be taking us off course a little, but I keep thinking about how you said earlier that you were part of the problem at Halton. Is that something you learned from The Collaborative Way?"

Caffey nodded. "Like I said, I was pretty angry after I lost my job. And being angry about it, I kept chewing on what happened, playing it over and over again in my mind. It's probably a good thing we didn't run into each other back then." He smiled ruefully. "I probably would have said some things I'd regret today. But as I practiced The Collaborative Way at Pinnacle, I gradually began to see what happened at Halton differently. I started seeing how I contributed to what happened and taking more and more responsibility."

I was impressed. "Can you give me some examples?"

"If you don't mind, Barry, I'd like to share examples as we get into some of the aspects of The Collaborative Way."

"That'll be interesting," I said. "It's pretty unusual for someone to take that kind of responsibility."

"I'm glad you brought this topic up, though. I left something important off the diagram. Let me add it." He wrote a few words and drew what looked like an arrowhead at the bottom of the diagram.

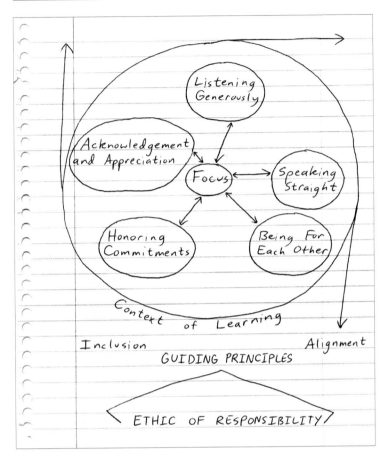

"As we say at Pinnacle, The Collaborative Way arises out of an Ethic of Responsibility. I find that as I practice The Collaborative Way, I'm taking more and more responsibility and ownership for what is happening around me, including what happened back at Halton and why I lost my job."

I raised my eyebrows at that. "As a CEO, that sounds too good to be true. How were you responsible for losing your job?"

"After Rycor bought us, I kept trying to do things the way we always did them at Halton—after all, we made a lot of money our way—and I resisted adapting to Rycor's way of doing things. They came to see me as an obstructionist and let me go."

I was impressed again. "That's amazing you could own up to that."

"It wasn't easy. It was a lot easier to blame you and Rycor, but being a victim wasn't getting me anywhere." Caffey turned to me, ready to get to work. "If you're up for it, Barry, let's look deeper into the practice of The Collaborative Way. I think what I'm talking about will begin to make sense to you. I thought we could start by looking at each of the five commitments in more detail. Obviously, we can only hit the high points in one afternoon."

"Sounds good," I said, but I wondered what I'd gotten myself into.

Today...

The big meeting was today. A lot of work had gone into the plan for the new strategic initiative I was presenting to our leadership team. We had invested a lot of time and money developing the plan. The vision I had for our company, what I had come to call "Zero Delay," depended on this plan moving forward.

The meeting couldn't have fallen on a better day. The coincidence seemed symbolic. It was Sonoran Communities' third anniversary of taking on The Collaborative Way. The huge step forward we were about to take would not have been possible without it. I thought about how it had all started when I ran into Caffey at my favorite restaurant a little over three years ago on a night when I had felt so discouraged about Sonoran's future. I had been ready to give up. I remembered the day we spent together, when he had shared how much he had grown from practicing The Collaborative Way, contrasting that to life at our first company, Halton Homes. I decided that day to bring this way of working together to Sonoran, and that decision initiated a profound change in my company and me.

I took a detour on my drive to see how work was coming on our Houghton development. As much as we had improved, there were still more guys standing around than I liked to see—a couple of them propped on shovels, a few sitting on tailgates. In the old days, I would have stopped the truck, got out and started yelling. But I had learned through my practice of The Collaborative Way that jumping to conclusions and getting on people about not doing what they are supposed to be doing does not get me what I want. I also knew from experience that they were probably waiting for a truck that was late, or there was some mistake that needed to get fixed before they could get back to work. That's what Zero Delay was about: getting rid of those inefficiencies. I wanted to take what companies in manufacturing had done and bring those same innovations to the construction world. I wanted Sonoran to become the benchmark for our industry.

CHAPTER ONE

LISTENING GENEROUSLY

A little over three years ago…

*C*affey pointed to the circle labeled "Listening Generously" on the diagram he had drawn. "Let's start here—the commitment to Listen Generously. This practice makes collaboration so much easier. I think both of us had a lot to learn about listening when we worked at Halton. I think this may be one of your blind spots, Barry."

I smiled. "You meant it when you said this could be hard. So, you don't think I was a good listener? I always listened to you."

"Sometimes. Most of the time. But I was one of the few people you seemed to listen to. I can remember going with you to one of our sites that wasn't making money and hearing you talk to the superintendent. Listening is not exactly the word I would use to describe what you were doing. Yelling, maybe. Screaming. Pissed off." We both laughed. "I remember you picking up a rock and throwing it so far I thought you might have set an Olympic record. You went in there certain about what that super was doing wrong and what he should do to fix it, and you made sure he heard what you had to say. You didn't care about listening to him."

I laughed. "I remember that time. I about killed my arm. But what did I need to listen to him for? I knew he was doing almost everything wrong, and I knew what he should do to fix it. I'd already been there a million times. I just needed him to fix things as fast as possible, so we could try to start making some money."

Caffey looked at me for a moment without saying anything. I could tell he was frustrated with me but trying not to act out of his frustration. I wondered if he was counting to ten in his head. Calmly, he answered, "Like I said, this is one of your blind spots. There are a lot of reasons for Listening Generously. One of them is so you don't have to go out for those kinds of meetings over and over again. When we aren't listening, we aren't building leaders. We aren't even building team players. We're just building yes-men—resentful ones at that. If you had listened, there just might have been something you could have learned. Let me ask you this: did your way of doing things work at Halton?"

"The sites started making money after I took over." I wasn't ready to roll over and just admit my way of doing things wasn't right.

"Sure. But did it work? Did you realize your vision for Halton? Are you still doing the same things at Sonoran?"

I didn't answer. I didn't like how pushy Caffey was being.

He could tell I was annoyed. "Are you open to having me talk to you like this? Being really straight and direct? I don't think anyone dared to talk to you like this when we worked together. But at Pinnacle people are encouraged to talk straight. It's part of being a team. I'm trying to give you the first step in doing something different—a tool that's been proven to work. It's worked for Pinnacle and it's worked for me."

"What do you mean? Just listen more? Just go out and listen to the complaints and excuses of every idiot I've hired?"

Caffey chuckled and shook his head. "First off, I don't think you've hired any idiots. And, yes, it might not be a bad idea to go out and listen to every person you've hired. But that still isn't enough. It's not just listening more. Sure, that's part of it, but that's really a by-product of a complete shift in how you relate to listening.

"Your most powerful asset as a leader is your ability to influence people's actions. Most leaders think speaking is the only tool they have to influence people — it seems obvious. A leader gives a speech or an order, and people act."

"Right. That's what it took to get those sites making money."

"Yeah, but you had to do it over and over. When you Listen Generously, you begin to see that listening, not speaking, is really your most powerful tool for influencing action. It transforms how you interact with people. If you really listen to someone, you can collaborate with them. Together, you can get what you want accomplished. It ends up being more effective — and more fun. It also inspires people. People are motivated when they've been listened to. Not listening to people kills any sense of teamwork."

This was sounding ridiculous. "So, I just go out and listen to them and build a sense of team," I said sarcastically. "We collaborate and everything's better. That's going to take so much time we'll be bankrupt by the time we've finished the first meeting!"

Caffey looked at me again without saying anything. He

let out a breath. Calmly again, he said, "It's one of the things Roy says a lot: 'Slow down to go faster.' I'm suggesting you're going to have to slow down and listen if you want Sonoran to get beyond this limit you've run into."

That hit too close. "I don't think you have any idea what it's going to take to have Sonoran succeed. I don't think you should sit there and tell me what I need to do. Just because things are going great for you, you think you've figured it all out." I was getting louder.

"All right, Barry. Maybe it's too much to talk about all this right now."

"No, I want to hear about it. I think I probably need to hear it. But I don't like feeling like you think you know everything. I don't like feeling like you're going to tell me what to do because I obviously don't have a clue."

"Well, at least it gives you an idea of what that super felt like and what a lot of other people who've worked for you feel like when you treat them the same way. You obviously don't like it."

"Obviously not," I snapped.

The dogs got off the couch and scooted away into another room, their tails tucked under them. Caffey called after them, "Jazz, Star, it's all right. We're not angry. Nobody's angry." He rolled his eyes. "They run off as soon as a conversation gets a little intense." He patted the cushion on his chair and called them, but they wouldn't come back. He turned back to me. "And no, I don't think I have it all figured out. I don't know all of what it's going to take to make Sonoran work. You're right. All I want to do is share something I've learned that has made a difference for me. And it looks like you're going through some of the same things I did when I first took this on. I also remember what was going on when we failed at Halton. I was there. But

I'm sorry if it sounded like I was trying to tell you I know exactly what you need to do. That's not what I mean."

"I know. I know that's not what you were doing. I'm sorry." I stretched my legs and ran a hand through my hair. "You're right. I'm not used to having someone talk to me like this. It's probably good for me." I sat up straighter. "Let's get back to it. Listening. OK, so I just listen to them."

Caffey squinted at me, "Are you sure?"

I nodded. "No more outbursts. I'm clear about what we're doing."

"OK. And I apologize, too. Maybe I was getting a little too preachy."

"You're not going to back off on me now, are you?" I teased.

"No, I promise I won't do that. OK, going back to what I said, it's not just listening more; it's listening more effectively. It's not our normal way of listening. I'm talking about listening with real curiosity and an intention to learn. This requires paying attention and setting aside our filters."

"What do you mean, 'setting aside filters'?"

"Filters are automatic ways of listening, like the thoughts that were running through your head while your super was talking. Things like 'He's wrong. I'm right. I know how to fix this. He's an idiot. We don't have time for this. We need to make money.' They're the automatic thoughts we have when we're listening to someone. Now, we're never going to get rid of those thoughts. But as we practice, we can get better and better at noticing them. We start to recognize that at some level we're always listening through filters. Once you catch yourself listening through a filter, you shift to being curious about what the person is actually saying and trying to learn from that person. It's not easy with all the filters that come up, especially when it's a confrontational conversation or when your business is at stake. But if you want to be a great leader and to build a team of leaders, you have to do it. Like I said, if you don't, you kill off the collaboration in your company and ultimately limit your success.

"Let me give you an example of a filter. When we worked at Halton, sometimes you would come out into the field, almost immediately get upset and then tell everyone what to do. I would listen to you through the filter 'Here he goes again. He hasn't even taken the time to really find out what's going on. Let's ride this out. He'll be gone soon, and we can get back to work.' Not exactly the best way to hear what you had to contribute to the situation."

"Yeah," I crossed my arms and shook my head a little, "but you were probably right. I was probably reacting to something I saw and not really taking in the whole situation."

"Even so, if I had listened to your concern and let you know I heard what was bothering you, I bet you would have cooled down, and we could have worked together to resolve the issue."

"Maybe. I can tell sometimes that a lot of what gets me upset is that it seems like no one understands or cares why I'm so concerned."

"So just imagine the difference I could have made in those situations if I had made sure you experienced being heard. I think my failure to listen to you is one of the ways I contributed to the wall we ran into at Halton."

I said, "I'm sure my lack of listening didn't help much either."

Caffey asked, "Can you think of a filter you had for me back then?"

"Let me think." For the first time, I had a different

perspective on that difficult time at Halton. I saw how I might have contributed to the problems. "I guess I listened to you through a filter when you would come to me with problems the field was having with a change I was trying to implement. I would think: 'Once again, Caffey is buying into the excuses and complaints in the field. Why can't he just get the change made?'"

Caffey nodded. "Great. Thanks for sharing that with me. I'm sure there were times when there was some truth—maybe a lot of truth—to that view. But what chance do you think you had of hearing that I was actually trying to work out a real issue that you hadn't taken into consideration, that I was trying to help you make the change happen faster and more effectively?"

I shrugged. "Probably none."

"Once we have a filter, we listen in a way that gathers more evidence for the filter. If we notice the filter we have the chance, or choice, to move it aside and bring some authentic curiosity to the conversation."

I was starting to understand. "And I'll bet that if I had done that, we could have been a lot more productive in making change happen. Even those times when you had bought into the whining and complaining, I could have been more effective in having you see that if I hadn't been listening to you through a filter."

Caffey grinned. "I think you're starting to see the power of Listening Generously."

"But I still feel there are some situations when it might be almost impossible to set aside those filters and listen with curiosity."

"It's very difficult sometimes," Caffey admitted. "But I've found a number of things help me. One is just waking up about filters, being aware. I'll bet you start to notice them more often now. Another is confirming that you are actually hearing what someone is intending to say. I do this by paraphrasing back to the other person what I thought I heard them say, to check if I'm getting it right. It's amazing how many times that reveals a misunderstanding."

I could feel my resistance creeping back in. "Do you constantly paraphrase during every conversation? Doesn't that seem awkward?"

"Of course not. I usually do it if I feel disturbed or confused by what I thought the other person said, or if I feel we have reached a commitment. Sometimes it does slow down the conversation, but again, it's that 'go slower to go faster' idea. If you reveal a misunderstanding early, it can sure save a lot of time later.

"I also work hard to appreciate where the other person is coming from. I try to walk a mile in their shoes. It helps your listening if you tell the person where you think they are coming from, what you see they are committed to accomplishing or how you think they're feeling. Checking in keeps me out of the trap of assuming I know. And in difficult conversations it can help release negative emotions."

I thought for a moment. "I guess I usually take whatever I think I hear someone say to be what they intended to say. Maybe that's a big assumption."

"And a potentially costly one. It's great you're seeing that," Caffey said. "So, along with paraphrasing and checking in with someone about where they're coming from, it's also essential to make sure you're listening with a willingness to be influenced. If you're not open to being influenced, you're not Listening Generously."

I made a face and shook my head a little. "You're saying I'm supposed to actually let someone I know is wrong influence me?" I stopped. "I'm sorry. I'm getting argumentative again. It just seems crazy."

"Of course, I don't mean you should let someone who is wrong tell you what to do. Listening Generously doesn't mean you end up agreeing with everyone all the time. It's not about becoming a soft person who just goes along with everything they hear. It's a way of approaching listening that opens up collaboration in whatever form that might take. The person might end up doing exactly what you wanted them to do. But if you take the time to listen first, it becomes collaboration instead of domination. For example, I know for a fact that a lot of those supers were not dead wrong idiots. You missed out on a lot by not listening to them."

"You're probably right," I agreed.

"It's a willingness to be influenced, not 'you will be influenced.' You've set aside your filters. You're being curious. You're not stuck in your position. You're ready to be influenced if that fits."

"That makes sense."

"Again, I know it may sound like I think I'm an expert at all of this, but I'm not. It's been hard for me, too. It's actually really good for me to go over it all with you, and I appreciate the way you're challenging what I'm saying. It helps me get clearer about it. I've found this stuff even works at home, too, especially with my daughter. Like I told you, she's sixteen now. You can imagine what that's like: the clothes, the attitude, the boyfriends. Things had gotten pretty bad between us. But I tried really listening to her—getting out of my filters and being curious, trying to learn how it was for her and definitely being willing to be influenced. It's worked out so well she even told Diane, 'I want to talk to Dad. He listens to me.' That really got Diane's attention," he laughed. "Diane said, 'She used to hate you. What's going on here?' She wanted to know what

I was doing differently, and when I explained, she started taking on Listening Generously herself. Now Mariah has two parents who listen to her. I wish I'd had that when I was a kid."

"It's hard for me to believe things got bad with Mariah—little Mariah?" I was remembering a little girl playing in a tree house in one of the big mesquite trees in their backyard.

Caffey rolled his eyes. "She's not so little anymore. You'll see when they get back. It was always easy for me to know what she should do and to tell her so. But it's the listening that's helped."

"Helen's told me so many times: 'Your problem, Barry, is that you just don't listen.' She'll love it when I tell her she was right."

We both laughed.

Caffey said, "It hasn't been easy to keep improving my listening. Sometimes it's hard work to listen to someone. And I admit that sometimes I do a lousy job of it. But I'm amazed at how often situations that seem really challenging work themselves out with a little listening."

Today...

I wasn't more than a few steps in the front door of our main office, and my general superintendent, Frank Bunch, was right there. I had a feeling the day of the big meeting was going to be challenging. Frank was an old-school guy. He had been with us since the beginning and had been working construction for years before that. The sun had weathered his skin to dry earth, and he was short and built like a brick house. He was exactly the kind of guy I needed to win over for Zero Delay to succeed.

Frank started walking down the hall with me. "I didn't want to ambush you in the meeting," he said, "but I need to talk to you about this plan. I've been thinking about it, and I still don't buy it. I think we're shooting ourselves in the foot with this. We've got a good thing going here, and I think we're getting greedy with this. This is construction. And this Zero Delay—" he huffed, "this 'bring the manufacturing world into construction' just doesn't sit right. This isn't manufacturing! Like it or not, we're not in a factory out there. I feel like this is the latest fancy management trend, and it's taking us off track."

I felt a knot twisting in my stomach. At this point, this was exactly the line of thinking that I was sick of. And the fact that Frank, who was on the leadership team, was bringing it up now—I felt ready to snap. I just wanted to overpower him and get him out of the way. We were still walking. I stopped. I knew I wouldn't get the results I wanted that way. I needed to listen to him to have any chance of fully gaining his support. "I'm glad you came to me before the meeting," I said. "Thank you." I wanted to make sure I understood what he was saying instead of assuming. I turned to him. "So, you're saying that because things have always been this way—and we're making good money this way—things should stay the way they are. That if we keep trying to get better, we're going to grab for too much, and it's going to be our undoing."

Frank nodded. "Yeah, basically. We're here to make money. I don't see how we're going to be making money spending all this time planning and organizing about how to do the job better. We already do the best job around. We need to be focusing on getting more business and keeping costs low, making more money. That should be our focus. We've already got high quality."

I could feel my automatic filters kicking in: I've already heard this before. I know how I'm going to rebut this. I'm right; he's wrong. I reminded myself of how important it was to listen to Frank, set these filters aside and keep being curious. "You feel like our focus should be on how to make the most money we can, not on how to get better in areas that don't directly relate to increasing profits."

"Exactly. It's like we're trying to get better for the sake of getting better. This whole Zero Delay plan book is total overkill. I could see it if we had people that didn't know what they were doing. But we don't. Our guys are all professionals. It's really an insult to them. And a couple of them have said as much. It's just not good business. We're wasting time with this thing." He threw up his hands. "This isn't a hobby! This is a business!"

I set aside the idea of winning the conversation and focused on being willing to be influenced by Frank. "OK, I see what you mean. It looks like the focus of Zero Delay is just to make us look better. It doesn't keep the focus on profit, which is where it should be. And that concerns you. You want this company to succeed. You're committed to our success. You see this as taking us down the wrong path."

He nodded. "Yeah, that's it." He looked at me. "You know, this is the first time I feel like you really got my point."

"I think so, too. To be honest, I feel like this is the first time I really listened to you about it."

"I could tell you were Listening Generously."

"Yeah, I noticed myself feeling frustrated at first, but I focused on listening to you, and I finally understood what you were trying to communicate. I just wish I had done a better job of listening sooner. So, do you feel like you could Listen Generously to me now?"

"Sure. Now that I feel like I finally got my point across, it'll probably be a lot easier."

He put his hands in his pockets, squared up with me and looked me in the eye. "I'm ready. Listening Generously." He was having fun with it. "Shoot."

"Zero Delay is about us making more money. It's not about making the most efficient work site just for the sake of it. If we can remove all the constraints we work under, or at least greatly reduce them, we'll be doing the job faster and with fewer mistakes. And that means more profit. With this plan, we're taking out the inconsistency in our work. I know we have some great people, and I know we have a reputation for high quality work, but there's still not enough consistency. Even though we've gotten a lot better, we still have a couple of sites here and there that don't make budget.

Zero Delay's going to bring all of our work up to where it should be. Then there won't be any reason for us not to continue to be the top homebuilding company in Tucson, no matter how competitive the market gets.

"We are here to make money," I continued. "You're absolutely right about that. And Zero Delay is the best way to take us to the next level."

Frank squared himself up again. "OK, let me try giving this back to you. You're saying that this whole thing isn't just a vanity project." He chuckled. "Because Zero Delay will have all the sites working as efficiently as they can, we will be making more money. It's going to get rid of the occasional bad site and have them all working faster and with fewer mistakes." Begrudgingly, he said, "I know it sounds obvious, but I still feel resistant to it."

"Why?"

"I don't know. It seems too simple. You can't just put construction into a formula. There are too many variables out there."

"I agree. There's still going to be a need for our best people to be out there running things. This is just going to make it a lot easier. And you know the joke: 'If superintendents were firefighters, they'd be arsonists.' We love to fight those fires, but that's just not the best way to run a company."

He nodded. "All right. I get it. I feel better about it. Once I felt like you'd finally listened to me, it was a lot easier to listen to you." He nodded again. "I know you've said all this before, but I guess I needed you to hear me out first."

I put my hand on his shoulder. "That's the Listening Generously principle: 'If you're not being heard, there's something you're not hearing.' I wasn't able to get my point across, so I needed to stop and listen to what you had to say first."

"All right, I don't want to start hugging. I've got work to do. I'll see you in the meeting."

I laughed and clapped him on the shoulder.

❖

As I walked back to my office, I imagined how that conversation would have gone before we had started working with The Collaborative Way. I probably would have told Frank that I was sick of his line of thinking, that I had gone over the reasons for what we were doing a dozen times before and, at this point, he just needed to trust me. I would have steamrolled past him and lost him as an ally. I would have created another person who felt excluded, resentful and devalued—my old standard operating procedure. I felt very grateful for all I'd learned by practicing Listening Generously. I was a better leader because of it.

CHAPTER TWO

SPEAKING
STRAIGHT

A little over three years ago…

*C*affey stood at his refrigerator as it crushed ice into his glass. He filled his glass with water and called over to me, "Do you want anything while I'm over here? Some more water?"

I said I was fine. I chided Caffey, "Are you still chewing ice?" He had just taken a drink.

He walked over, chewing a piece and smiling as he sat on the couch. He finished chewing and said, "Maybe not as much as when you last saw me. I've tried to cut back a little."

I raised my eyebrows and wagged my finger at him jokingly, "It's going to crack your teeth."

He shrugged. "They're holding up so far. Maybe I've been blessed with extra strong teeth genes to compensate for my addiction. It runs in the family. My dad still chews ice and has healthy teeth to show for it."

I laughed. "Maybe you're in luck. I hope so." I was still holding the diagram he had drawn. "Speaking Straight is next, right? I think I've already got this one down. You ever know me to pull any punches?"

Caffey laughed. "Well, it's not exactly that simple, and,

actually, I have known you to pull some punches. You yourself said one of the things you learned from your experience at Halton was that sometimes you didn't intervene early enough. You let situations drag on at times."

I rolled my eyes. "Here we go again. I thought this was going to be my strong suit."

"This one might not be so bad," he reassured me. "You are great at speaking up. That's a hallmark of us construction bosses—we tell it like it is. If someone's doing a lousy job, we let him know about it. And that's great. But the challenge is to build a company where everyone, not just the top executives, is encouraged to speak up. A place where everyone's supported in speaking up, whether it's to the people who work under them, to their peers or even to their bosses."

"I do that! I always encourage my guys to speak up. I always tell them to let me know if I'm doing something wrong. I tell them they're my eyes and ears out in the field, and they need to let me know what's really going on out there."

"You may be asking them to speak up, but when they see you not listening or blowing up on people, they get the message that you don't really want to hear what they have to say; it's not safe to tell you how it is. Why take the risk?

"When I felt you were locked down on a position, I usually wouldn't speak up. I'd think, 'Barry's a bright guy. He must know what he's doing. He's probably not going to listen to me anyway. Maybe I'll hit a sore spot, and he'll go off on me. Why bother?'"

I felt a little disheartened. "So, I guess all those speeches about being my eyes and ears in the field were a waste of time. If I'm not going to listen, even when I think I've already got it all figured out, there's no point in asking them to speak up."

Caffey slapped the edge of the couch. "That's exactly right. And the real cost is that you miss out on a lot of what people have to contribute to the success of your company. I know I wasn't giving you the advantage of my perspective on the situation when I didn't speak up. I didn't want to go through the discomfort of having a difficult conversation with you. It's one of the things we work hard on at Pinnacle, encouraging people to speak upwards in the company."

"So, if I get the listening in place, I'll have my people telling me what's really going on. That's what I always wanted." I was starting to get it. "And if they're speaking upwards, I'll get their contribution. I always wanted that, too. It seems so obvious when you lay it out like that. It all seems like common sense."

"Most of it is — not all of it — but it sure isn't common practice. And that's the opportunity, to have it become common practice. But you want to encourage your people to do more than just speak up. You want to encourage them to speak up in a way that's honest and 'forwarding.'"

I scowled. I hadn't heard that term before. "What do you mean by 'forwarding'?"

"Forwarding means speaking in a way that gets you closer to what you're committed to accomplishing. It's speaking in a way that makes a contribution. You might be speaking honestly, but you're not Speaking Straight if you're not making a contribution. Just dumping your judgments and assessments on someone is not Speaking Straight, and it isn't getting you any closer to having a great company."

"Just so I'm clear," I said, "I can still have hardnosed conversations with people as long as I make sure I'm contributing and moving things forward?"

"Absolutely. If you're not having those difficult

conversations when you need to, you're not Speaking Straight. But in difficult conversations it's important to make sure your speaking is rigorous. I struggle with this sometimes. I get sloppy and fail to distinguish between the facts about an issue and my opinions about it. I start stating my opinions as facts, and that tends to shut down the conversation. It makes it especially hard to collaborate when I'm telling the other person my opinion as if it's a fact, and the other person doesn't see things the same way as I do, which is usually the case in a difficult conversation."

I leaned forward in my chair. "I have a construction manager who needs to hear this. I know he avoids difficult conversations. He's always complaining to me about his people not getting things done, but whenever I ask him if he's talked to them, the answer's almost always no."

"It also sounds to me like he's having a problem with making clear and direct requests," Caffey said. "It's amazing how many times we don't get what we're asking for because we do a poor job of making a request. It's easy to walk away from an interaction thinking someone has agreed to do something. But when you look back on it, you can see that either you weren't really clear regarding what you were asking for or you didn't get a specific time by when it would get done. You may not have really gotten the other person's agreement to do what you were asking. You just assumed you did."

I knew what he was talking about. "You mean you don't settle for answers like 'I'll try' or 'let me think about it.'"

"You're begging for problems if you do."

The two dogs poked their heads back into the room. Caffey patted the couch and called them over. "Everything's happy in here. You can come out now." Tails wagging, they came around the corner. "Diane would love it if we took them for a W-A-L-K. I can't say it or they'll get crazy."

"A walk—oops—a W-A-L-K sounds great. I feel like I've been sitting all day."

The dogs were jumping on Caffey's lap and trying to lick his face. "Hold on." He pushed them onto the couch. "We're going to take care of you. Just wait a second." They stared at us with their tongues hanging out. "I've just got one more thing to tell Barry about Speaking Straight."

"When you're encouraging your people to speak up, I think it's important to appreciate how uncomfortable it can be to speak straight. You have to really be willing to risk being uncomfortable to bring up those tough, potentially confrontational issues. Especially when you think the other person might get upset. I bet even for someone like you, who usually has no problem speaking up, there are times when it's uncomfortable. If you're not careful, that discomfort can stop you from Speaking Straight and dealing with the issues that need to be dealt with. You said you didn't intervene soon enough at Halton. I'll bet in some way that was related to being uncomfortable."

Jazz pawed at Caffey's leg and stared at him. "All right, mutts. Who wants to go for a walk?"

Today…

I waved and said good morning to my assistant, Estelle, and went into my office. Not two minutes after I sat down, the phone rang.

"Hey, Barry."

"Frank?" I was surprised to be hearing from him again so soon. I hoped he hadn't changed his mind about Zero Delay.

"I've been thinking about our conversation."

"The one we had five minutes ago about Zero Delay?"

"Don't worry," he said. "I'm still with you. I get how good Zero Delay's going to be for us. What I was thinking about was how easy it was for me to really listen to you and to get behind Zero Delay once I felt like my concerns were listened to. There are two superintendents, my buddies Mike Bullard and Aaron Phillips, who I know have some of the same concerns. And I hate to admit it — it's definitely not Being For Each Other — but we've sat around and had some doozies at Zero Delay's expense. But I know if you really listened to them, and you guys had a conversation like the one we had, you could help them work through their issues. I know they could get behind Zero Delay. But I think it's really important that you do it."

"Some doozies, huh?" I asked.

"Yeah. Some of them got pretty bad." We both laughed.

"I appreciate you giving me the heads up," I said. "I'll talk to both of them." I opened my calendar. "Anything else?"

"Well, I'd like to get a commitment on when you'll talk to them, Boss. Not to press you, but as you know, we don't have anything until I get a time by when it'll be done."

Even though we had been practicing Speaking Straight at Sonoran for three years, it still caught me off guard when someone pushed on me to be more rigorous in my commitments. I was the CEO. I had always gotten away with saying, 'Sure, I'll do that,' or, 'Sounds good.' Part of me wanted to tell Frank I could take care of it without giving him a time by when I would have it done; the other part was jumping up and down, celebrating the fact that he was Speaking Straight to me. We had worked so hard to make speaking straight a company-wide reality, and here it was. I pulled myself together. "You're absolutely right, Frank." I flipped through my calendar. "Let me take a look." I scanned through my appointments. "There's no way I can do it today."

"No, I know. Not with the meeting."

"I could do it tomorrow or the next day, though. I can commit to having talked to both of them by the end of the week."

"Can you commit to having gotten their support by the end of the week?"

I had to smile. I was proud of the culture we'd created — one where Frank felt comfortable enough to push me like this — even when it left me without the protection a CEO normally enjoys. It wasn't easy when you had to either back down or take the leap and commit. "You're pushing me on this. I appreciate that. OK, their support is what we're trying to get here, not just a conversation. I'll tell you what, I'll commit to having gained their support by the end of the day Monday—in case I hit a snag and need to talk more with either one of them." I realized I was making a commitment that I might fail to keep. I could make the safe commitment to just talk to them. That was one I knew I could keep. But what really mattered was getting these guys' support. Frank was right, and I knew I needed to risk failing. The risk of failure is a part of so many of the really important commitments we make.

I heard Frank let out a breath. I knew that hadn't been easy for him. "Thanks, Boss. If you need any help with either one, just give me a call."

"I will. Thanks for the offer. I may need it."

"I appreciate you being willing to make this commitment."

"You're welcome," I said. "And I liked the way you pushed me to take a risk and commit to what really mattered here."

"You're the first boss I've ever had that I felt OK pushing on. I'm just grateful to be working here. By the way, will you let me know as soon as you get their support?"

"Sure. I'll give you a call before the end of the day Monday."

We hung up and I leaned back in my chair. That never would have happened before The Collaborative Way. Frank never would have pushed me like that. And if he had, I would have told him it was none of his business. I'd take care of it. Back then I always had to be on top and in control. I was always the leader and never needed anyone's support. That control had been hard for me to let go of. It was one of the toughest things for me about The Collaborative Way. But it was clear how much Sonoran and I had gained. I wasn't the only one making things happen anymore. I wasn't the only leader. With the competition we faced and the need for change, I couldn't do it all by myself. We never would have gotten to the level of success we'd reached without there being leaders throughout Sonoran.

CHAPTER THREE

BEING FOR
EACH OTHER

A little over three years ago...

*I*t was March and already warm. I'd borrowed a hat from Caffey. We walked the dogs on leashes to where the street dead-ended at the desert preserve. Caffey picked a trail that curved into a wash. "This trail goes around the backside of that mountain and loops back to here." We let the dogs off their leashes and they ran ahead, sniffing bushes and putting their noses to holes in the ground.

I took the diagram Caffey had drawn out of my pocket as I followed him down into the wash. "Being For Each Other is next on the diagram," I said. "Is that like rooting for each other?"

"That's definitely a part of it. It basically means supporting each other's success."

That was something I felt strongly about. "I've always tried to do that. I've always been committed to supporting my people's success. In fact, I think I've done well in that area."

"I would agree. That's what you did for me. That's why I acknowledged you. Before I met you I had no idea what kind of leader I was capable of being. You're really good at seeing people's potential and encouraging them to step out and grow, which is so important in supporting success."

I thought about what I'd learned so far that day. "Thanks. But I'm beginning to see I'm not very good at handling breakdowns. That's when I could be better at supporting people's success. I already see how I could listen and speak more effectively instead of being so reactive in those situations."

"Imagine if you came to those breakdowns looking for the other person's positive intent," Caffey said. "That's Being for Each Other. Whoever was involved in the breakdown wasn't trying to screw up. Almost always the other person was trying to contribute. When you start from that point of view, you have a more powerful place to work from. Instead of treating the other person like they're trying to cause a problem and invalidating them, you use the opportunity as a chance to build them up."

I could tell I wasn't resisting the ideas Caffey was sharing with me anymore. They were all starting to make sense. "I bet it makes it much easier for him to hear what I'm trying to say if I come to the conversation with supporting him as part of my goal."

"Exactly. And when everyone in your company relates to each other like this, breakdowns become opportunities for people to support each other."

"That sounds like a great place to work." I patted one of the dogs that had stopped on the path to sniff under a rock. "A breakdown wouldn't be such a bad thing anymore!"

Caffey pulled a seedpod off a mesquite tree as he walked by it. The tree limb swung back and swayed. "That's the kind of culture we're building at Pinnacle. And again, we're not perfect at it by any means, but this is the common practice we've put in place and our declared way of working together."

We came up out of the wash and onto a trail that cut through a maze of creosote. Caffey stopped and peeled open the seedpod and collected the seeds in his hand. He tossed the pod off the trail. I looked out at the mountain range that half-circled this side of the preserve. Caffey said, "In the same way avoiding difficult conversations is a failure to speak straight, not handling performance issues is a common way people fail to be for each other. A lot of times people would just rather not address performance issues. I have a perfect example from back at Halton. It bothered me then and I still don't like it. There was this guy that we fired, Charles Bowen. He was one of my guys. He had a lot of talent, a lot of drive and he was loyal. I didn't like having to fire him, but by the time we finally talked to him, things had gotten so bad he didn't have any chance of turning them around. As we were getting ready to fire him, I looked back through all of the performance reviews I'd done on him. They were all positive and they shouldn't have been. Even back then, I could see how I had failed him. I wasn't willing to be uncomfortable and support him in dealing with his performance issues early on. I wanted to be his friend, so I let him slide a little. Looking through all those positive reviews, I felt horrible. I felt responsible for him getting fired. I've worked hard to never put myself in that position again."

I nodded. "I remember Charles. I remember the potential we saw in him. I can understand how painful it must have been to fire him after you realized you'd failed to support him."

Caffey motioned us forward and we started walking again. He said, "It motivates me to make sure it never happens again. If any of my employees have performance issues now, I bring them up as quickly as possible. Early on is your best opportunity to be supportive and to do something proactive about the issues. If you let things go too long, you're forced to be reactive, like I was with Charles. I wanted to be a nice guy and let things slide, but it didn't end up working for him at all."

I said, "I can think of times when I've waited until my doubts about someone were proven right, and it made the conversation a lot easier for me. But I can see now that it definitely didn't support the other person's success."

"That's great you already recognize that about yourself. Now that you know that's your tendency, you can do something about it. It's just like catching yourself in a filter when you're trying to Listen Generously." Caffey tossed the handful of mesquite seeds ahead of one of the dogs that was walking underfoot. He told her to hurry up. "Go on, Star. Run! We're out here to get you some exercise." He patted Star on the backside and she jogged ahead. Caffey said, "I want to make sure you're clear that you can fire someone while still being for them. It's just the way Charles was fired that made it not an expression of being for him. What makes the difference is the stance you fire someone from: out of support for their success and the success of the people around them. If you don't re-assign or fire someone who needs to be, you're not supporting their success or the success of the people who work with them."

Caffey continued, "I think people sometimes get confused and think supporting someone's success means just being nice to them. It's a much tougher and more meaningful way of relating than that."

We were almost to the mountain we were going to loop around. We could hear two people coming towards us. Caffey called the dogs back and held them both by the collars as a man and a woman came out from behind the mountain. As they walked by us, we all said hello.

❖

We passed into the shade on the other side of the mountain, and I took my hat off. Everything Caffey had said was rolling around in my head. I said, "I've found the hardest conversations, the ones I tend to avoid the most, are the conversations about something someone's done that has upset me. It's embarrassing for me to admit that I'm upset, and it's really uncomfortable to talk about it. The first few words are the worst. I usually just try to find a way to deal with the situation without talking to the person first."

"It's great you brought that up," Caffey said. "That's a big part of being for someone — being willing to have that kind of difficult conversation. If you don't have that conversation, you're not going to be able to continue to support the other person's success. Any issue that you leave unresolved is going to lead to problems between the two of you.

"We call that kind of conversation a 'clean up.' When you don't do a necessary clean up, you end up with a filter about the person, like the filters we talked about with Listening Generously. You're not able to work together as well anymore. And you'll probably end up gossiping about them, too. If an unresolved issue lingers, it's hard not to vent to someone about it. Then you start spreading your filter about them. But when Being For Each Other is a common practice, it's great how the person you vent to will re-direct you to do a clean up. I've had that happen a number of times."

I was a little skeptical. "You mean people actually tell each other to stop gossiping?"

"Not just to stop gossiping but to go and resolve the issue — to go do a clean up."

"Wow," I said. "I'm impressed."

"When you've got people taking a stand for each other, they won't let that kind of thing go on. And if it's necessary, they'll even push you to go apologize to the person you're gossiping about."

I stopped on the trail. "That would be asking a lot of me, Caffey. I've always viewed apologizing at work as a sign of weakness."

Caffey stopped ahead of me and turned around. He smiled. "I remember that about you. But an authentic apology is actually an expression of strength, not weakness. Look, doing what's necessary to make sure you have the best working relationships possible is a sign of strong leadership. I understand how hard it is to get yourself to do a clean up, regardless of whether it means you need to apologize or not. Even with everyone at Pinnacle practicing Being For Each Other, I still have to move through a lot of discomfort. But I'm clear about how important it is, and it motivates me to take that first step."

Today...

*E*stelle's voice came over the intercom, "Dan Osborn's here and he wants to talk to you. He says it's kind of important. Your schedule's open right now."

"Sure." I wondered what he wanted. "Send him in."

Dan came in, nodded and half-smiled. I could tell something was bothering him. He kept looking away from me like he didn't want to look me in the eyes. I asked him to sit down.

"Thanks for seeing me." He sat down and let out a long breath. "There's something I need to talk to you about."

"Sure. What would you like to talk about?"

He rubbed the back of his neck. I sat down across from him at the small table I used for meetings. Dan said, "First, I wanted to say that I'm here because I value our working relationship. I like working for you and I want it to stay that way. I'm committed to us having a great working relationship."

"I am, too. What's going on?" I was starting to worry.

He glanced at me and then traced the wood grain of the table. "I just found out this morning that you went around me yesterday and told my foremen to go ahead with the changes we talked about. I got to the site this morning, and the crews were already setting up to work on them."

I felt relieved. Dan's problem didn't seem like a big deal. "Yeah, with the deadline we're running there, I didn't feel like we could wait anymore. We talked about those changes several days ago. And when I checked, you hadn't done anything about it. I figured we'd already agreed on it. It didn't seem like a problem."

Dan looked up from tracing another grain in the wood. "I feel like you undermined my authority with my crews when you went around me like that. I'm telling them to do one thing, and then you come in and tell them to change the whole sequence. It sends a confusing message about whose instructions they're supposed to follow. I already had detailed plans in line with the Zero Delay ideas, and I spent a lot of time working in these last minute changes. I had it planned out so the changes wouldn't cause any delays, and then you go and tell the crews to make the changes right now. It threw off all my work. When I found out I thought, 'Why do all this planning if Barry's going to come around and change things anyway?' I know that's not your intent. I know you were just trying to make sure we hit our deadline. But I think it's important for you to know the kind of impact you have when you go and do something like that."

He looked straight at me. "Why didn't you just come to me? I don't understand. I found myself doubting your support for me. If you didn't feel like I was moving fast enough why didn't you just tell me?"

I said, "I did it because we've got to make our deadlines," but I knew I'd made a mistake. It was obvious. I had acted without really thinking about Dan, and I had ended up getting in the way of all his hard work. I turned up my hands. "I guess I lapsed back into my old ways of doing things, just taking over. Old habits die hard, especially when there's a deadline. We can't start missing deadlines. But you're absolutely right. It was a lapse in my support for you. I reacted to my interpretation of what was happening without addressing my concerns to you. I let my fear of not making the deadline take over and made a mess of things. I apologize. I hope it doesn't mess things up too badly for you."

"I'll make it work. And thanks for saying that, Barry."

I turned up my hands again. "I messed up. And I can see that I didn't really make a clear and direct request at the beginning. I didn't set a clear time by when I wanted those changes put in place or tell you why the timing was important to me. I'll work on being clearer in my requests."

Dan sat up straighter, like a burden had been lifted from his shoulders. "Fair enough. And I'll try to be more sensitive about finding out what your time requirements are. When I'm doing my planning, I'll get in touch with you right away if the requirements cause an issue, so we can work it out together. That way you won't end up being surprised."

"That's great, Dan. And I really appreciate you coming in here. The last thing I want to do is discourage someone who has the kind of commitment to our success that you have. I'm shooting myself in the foot if I'm not supporting you."

"Is that a promise, Barry?" Dan had a hint of a smile, but he was serious. "Can you commit to talking to me before you intervene in one of my projects again?"

"Definitely. I commit to talking to you before I step in again."

Dan stood up. "I feel a lot better. I'm ready to get back to work. I'm glad I came in here and cleaned this up with you. This is the first place I've ever worked where I could work out a problem with my boss like this."

"This is what Being For Each Other looks like." I felt like giving Dan a high five, but I thanked him again instead, and we shook hands. We were both smiling, enjoying what we'd accomplished.

❖

After Dan left, I thought back to that conversation I had had with my old friend Caffey more than three years ago. Collaborative Way anniversaries always remind me of him. If only he could see me now—he wouldn't even recognize me! I let people support me now. I let someone tell me when I did something wrong! And I thanked him for it! I shook my head. It was hard to believe how far I had come.

Sonoran felt like a team now. Like Caffey had said, we were working together to reach our goal. We didn't let our conflicts and upsets get in the way. We used them to bring us closer together. I was proud of how we worked together and excited about what we could accomplish.

CHAPTER FOUR

HONORING COMMITMENTS

A little over three years ago…

We rounded the mountain and came out into the bright light. It had been a hike up the backside, and I was a little out of breath. The dogs were off the path and out of sight. We jogged down a slope of loose rocks and stopped at the bottom.

"No rest for the weary," I said, smiling. I put my borrowed hat back on and took the diagram out of my pocket again. "Honoring Commitments. Does that just mean do what you say you're going to do?"

As we followed the trail down into another wash, Caffey said, "Yes, and it's more than that, too. It's being responsible for the commitments you participate in, whether you're the one who makes the commitment or the one who receives it. The idea that the receiver of a commitment has any responsibility is something I had no concept of back at Halton."

I teased Caffey, "I like hearing you were less than perfect, too. It makes me feel a little better."

Caffey chuckled. "I was far from perfect. I was a big part of our inability to keep our commitments. So often back at Halton, someone would make a commitment to me, and

I would say to myself, 'I bet he's not going to do that. He won't get it done. He never comes through.' I've learned how destructive that kind of thinking is. Being a responsible receiver of a commitment means that I only accept commitments I think will be kept. I deal with any issues or concerns I have up front instead of waiting to find out if I'm right. I recognize that a commitment someone makes to me is my commitment, too. Honoring that commitment means I have to be committed that it's going to happen.

"It also requires that I continue to support the other person, like checking in with them if I start to have a concern about whether or not the commitment is going to be kept. I might find out everything's fine. But if not, I can help them recover their commitment, get them any additional resources they might need and possibly even make alterations to the commitment. That kind of checking in makes a huge difference. It's way more powerful than the attitude 'They just don't keep their commitments.' That's being a victim."

I was trying to get my head around this new way of looking at commitments. We ducked under the overgrowth from two palo verde trees that covered the path through the wash. As we hunched over and made our way through, I asked, "So it's all about the receiver?"

Caffey stopped on the other side of the palo verdes. "It's not all about the receiver. That's just the part I had no concept of before. On both sides, though, it's about responsibility. And like you said, first and foremost is simply keeping your commitments, moving towards an 'it will happen' mentality."

"That's how I relate to my commitments," I said. "I find a way to make them happen, even when obstacles come up. I don't let reasons and excuses or changing circumstances stop me."

Caffey nodded. "You've got that 'it will happen' mentality ingrained in you, and that's great. But even if you're really good at keeping your commitments, Honoring Commitments also includes noticing as soon as you switch mentally from 'it will happen' to just wishing or hoping that it'll happen. If there's a problem, you immediately get back in touch with the person you made the commitment to and work it out with them. You don't just wait to see if you can keep the commitment before you get back to them." Caffey motioned. "Let's keep walking."

I could see the value of that. As I followed Caffey I said, "That addresses one of my big complaints: people wait until after the deadline to let me know that a commitment hasn't been kept, at which point there's nothing I can do about it. Or worse yet, sometimes they don't say anything about it not being kept until I bring it up. But I can see that if I share in a commitment someone makes to me, it would be easier and more natural for them to share any doubts about whether or not they're going to be able to keep it. It makes more sense if they see the commitment as something we're in on together."

Caffey gestured with his fist. "Exactly! That's what Honoring Commitments is about. You both share in the responsibility for a commitment. You're a team. It's great that you could see that. A lot of people who are really good at keeping commitments, like I know you are, have difficulty giving up that Lone Ranger mentality — the idea that once you make a commitment, it's all on you; you're on your own. That mentality is what keeps people from speaking up about problems early on in the commitment."

I agreed. "And I can see that by making both parties responsible for a commitment, you put a much stronger structure in place for having commitments kept. It makes a lot of sense."

The path came out of the wash, and we walked along a wire fence at the edge of the preserve. We could see into the backyards of the houses on the other side of the fence. They all had pools. The dogs fell into a line in front of us.

"And it's not like we're perfect at Pinnacle," Caffey said. "No one's going to be. After ten years of practicing, we still have broken agreements. But we make sure we deal with them. It's not Honoring Commitments if you ignore it when people don't do what they said they would. You call them on the commitments they break and hold them accountable for any consequences. But you don't beat them up about it and make them out to be bad people for it. You don't use their commitments to demean them. That's not supporting them. Along with responsibility, Honoring Commitments is about supporting people. What's important is that you get a new commitment when it's clear a commitment hasn't been kept, and you make sure there's support in place, so it's kept this time. You put whatever you need to in place to make sure it gets done, and you move forward."

I groaned. "That's tough to realize. I can see that I've used the commitments people have made to me almost like a club in my push to make things happen. I've also ignored broken commitments and just worked around people to get things done. It works sometimes, but no wonder no one lets me know when a commitment is in danger. Who wants to get beat up on? And no wonder people try to avoid making commitments altogether. It's not a very supportive environment and not really an expression of being for the other person's success." I took the diagram out again and studied it for a minute. "I'm starting to understand how the commitments that make up the Collaborative Way work together and support each other."

Caffey nodded and said, "I like to think of them like spokes of a wheel. They're all mutually reinforcing. If any one of them is weak or missing, the wheel's going to eventually fall apart."

The path took us back down into the wash we had started our hike in. Caffey said, "There are two other commitment pitfalls that Honoring Commitments addresses. The first has to do with trying to remember all your commitments. No matter how good your memory is, it's essential that you write them down and keep track of them."

Finally, something I was good at! "That's why I carry my notepad with me all the time."

"You're already on top of that one. The other pitfall is that people have the tendency to say yes to any commitment that's asked of them. Even though it's hard to say no, you have to remember that the whole reason we make commitments is to help us reach our goals. You only want to make commitments that contribute to your company's goals and vision. And you obviously don't say yes to commitments that you're not going to be able to fulfill because you don't have the resources or time. You don't just say yes to every request that comes your way."

I chuckled. "I look forward to that conversation — the day someone tells me, "No, that commitment you're asking me to make isn't forwarding to what we're committed to accomplishing.'"

Caffey chuckled, too. "That sounds like someone I'd like to hire."

Today...

*E*stelle buzzed the intercom. "Roberta Cole is here for her appointment."

"Send her in." Roberta was the construction manager overseeing the Houghton development.

I stood and we shook hands. I motioned her to have a seat. "Roberta," I said, "I've got two customer requests that made their way to me. Two families say they need to move in earlier than the date they agreed to. They're willing to pay extra, but they really need to move in sooner. It's something about the sales of their houses."

Roberta leaned forward. "Which two are they?"

I looked through my papers. "House four and house nine."

She made a face. "House four is a long way from done."

"I didn't promise them anything, and we're not going to compromise the grand opening date for the whole community. We haven't missed an opening date in three years, and I'm very proud of that."

"I agree." Roberta nodded. "When do they want to move in by?"

"House nine by August 7th, and House four by September 21st."

She relaxed a little. "Well, that's better. Let me think."

She looked up at the ceiling and mumbled to herself as she thought things through. "I think we can do it. Yeah, we can do it."

I was a little surprised. "And not compromise our opening date?"

"Yeah."

I let out a breath and leaned back in my chair. "I'm a little worried about how easily you answered that. You can make a commitment to have those two houses ready by those dates and still have the community opening of November 1st?"

"Yeah, Barry, I can. I'll have House nine ready by August 7th, House four by September 21st and have the entire community ready by November 1st."

"Well, that's impressive! You'll let me know if anything comes up that could jeopardize your commitment?"

"Absolutely."

"Great." We both stood up. "Again, I'm impressed. I expected this to be just a formality, so I could tell the customers that I looked into it, but we weren't going to be able to accommodate them. They'll be thrilled."

❖

As soon as Roberta left, my mind went back to the days when Sonoran was piling delay upon delay. Back then, we missed a number of grand opening dates. No one would even warn me about an impending delay until a few days before the deadline. It was as if they were trying to hide it from me. I treated the situation like it was all out of my hands. I made my employees out to be bad people who couldn't keep commitments. There wasn't anything I could do about it except fire everybody.

But since we'd taken on The Collaborative Way, I saw

what a victim I had been—just like Caffey had told me. I had learned how to effectively request commitments, like I had just done with Roberta, and how to support people in keeping them. I had learned how to be responsible for the commitments I participated in. I was definitely going to check in with Roberta, looking for ways to support her, and I knew she would keep me informed if there was any real danger of her commitment not being kept.

❖

I had scheduled a meeting with one of my superintendents, Evan Rich, out at the Tanque Verde site. It was a meeting I never would have bothered with if I hadn't developed a sense of Honoring Commitments. I had a suspicion that Evan wasn't on track to keep a commitment he'd made to me. I could have talked to him on the phone about it, but it was a discussion I thought we needed to have in person.

In the past, just like with the site delays, I would have waited out my suspicion and let Evan succeed or fail on his own. If he failed, I would have used his failure as further evidence of his inability to keep commitments and made him out to be someone I couldn't count on. Back then, I had no concept of supporting someone in keeping their commitments. The way I thought of it, once you made a commitment you were on your own. I used commitments to test people's drive to succeed. It was no wonder Sonoran used to have so many problems with its commitments.

❖

I found Evan talking to one of his foremen next to a nearly finished home. He wrapped up his conversation, and we stepped into the shade of the garage.

I said, "I'm here because I checked with the other people on the Zero Delay committee, and no one's heard anything from you about your proposal. Nothing's been scheduled with any of us. I started to get a little worried, so I thought I'd drop by and see what was up."

Evan took his cap off and ran a hand through his hair. "Yeah, I've just been swamped with wrapping up this site and getting ready for today's meeting. I haven't had any time to devote to it."

"Well, we're all still operating under the understanding that you're going to be ready to present to us by the end of next week."

"Maybe we should put it off," he said. "I'm so far behind on it I don't know if I'm going to be ready by then."

I could feel myself getting upset. I didn't need to come all the way out to his site just to find out that he wasn't sure he was going to be ready with his proposal on time! He didn't even seem concerned about not keeping his commitment. If I hadn't come to check up on him, I probably would have had to call him at the end of next week to find out he wasn't going to keep his commitment. On top of it all, this wasn't the first time with Evan. I was ready to hammer him down with everything he was doing wrong, but I stopped. I knew it wouldn't get me what I wanted. What I really wanted—and what Sonoran needed—was for Evan to succeed. I wanted to honor the commitment he'd made—honor our commitment. That was the more powerful way of looking at it.

I took a deep breath. "We could do that, but I'm concerned it's starting to look like a pattern where you don't follow through on the great ideas you come up with. This proposal could be a really important first win for Zero Delay. When you first presented your ideas for cutting time off our foundation laying process, I got really excited. It was great how you jumped right in, looking to see where we could implement Zero Delay. That's the kind of drive it's going to take to make Zero Delay work and to accomplish our vision. But if we let this first win fall off course, it's going to hamper the whole process of implementation." I stopped to look directly at him for a moment. "Besides that, Evan, this is a powerful opportunity for you to break this pattern that's starting to emerge."

He moved some of the landscape gravel around with his foot. "You might be right about the pattern. I didn't really want to admit it, but I've been thinking about it, too. Since I've been so busy, I felt justified in not getting the proposal done on time. But I think that's the excuse I've always used." He put his cap back on and looked at me. "All right. I'll get it done. I'll have it ready by next week. I'll just have to put in some work this weekend, but I'll have it done."

"Great. Is there anything I can do to support you?"

Evan shook his head. "Just bringing it up like you have. I'll get it done now."

"When are you going to schedule the meeting?" I asked. "If you wait until the middle of next week to set it up, we're not all going to be available."

"I'll call everyone as soon as we're done here."

"To help you out, I checked with everybody. We're available to meet from three to five next Thursday. Will that work for you?"

He patted the landscape gravel smooth again with his foot. "OK, I'll make that work." He looked up at me. "Thanks for doing that."

"You're confident you're going to be ready by next Thursday?"

"I'll do whatever it takes."

I was excited Evan was stepping up as a leader like this. "This is going to be an important first step for Zero Delay. I really want to see you succeed with this, Evan. You have great ideas, and I know you can be a real leader."

"Thank you. Thanks for supporting me. As much as I was dreading this conversation, I know you're here to support me in keeping my commitments. I appreciate that."

"You're welcome. And if you ever think you're not going to be able to keep a commitment, don't wait to bring it up. It makes it a lot easier to get you the support you need if you bring it up right away. It's easier to deal with the issue and make necessary changes if you don't wait until we're right at the deadline, and we have to struggle to recoup. It's all a part of honoring your commitment. And I really appreciate you being willing to put in the extra work to honor your commitment."

CHAPTER FIVE

ACKNOWLEDGMENT
AND
APPRECIATION

A little over three years ago…

We came off the trail back onto the street that dead-ended at the preserve. Caffey called the dogs, and we put them back on their leashes.

"We're on the last commitment," I said. I looked at the diagram. "Acknowledgment and Appreciation." I groaned. "I'm no good at this one. I already know that."

"I used to be horrible at it, too," Caffey said. "I don't think it's natural for some people to give acknowledgment and show appreciation. It's too uncomfortable."

I offered to take one of the leashes from Caffey, and we started down the street. I said, "It feels fake to me. I can force a 'good job,' but anything beyond that is just not in my nature. I expect people to do what they're supposed to do. I expect them to get the job done no matter what. That's what I expect of myself. But then it ends up backwards. I end up giving all my attention to the people not doing what they're supposed to be doing."

"Negative reinforcement," Caffey said.

"Yeah. I know positive reinforcement is the thing to do. It's just so much easier to see what's wrong or what's not working. It feels like there's so much being done wrong it's all I have time to deal with."

"What I've had to do is treat acknowledgment like a commitment—a commitment you make to acknowledge and appreciate the people you work with. The first step to fulfilling this commitment is to start noticing and seizing the opportunities as they come along. I know some people at Pinnacle who put 'give acknowledgment' on their to-do lists every day. You just have to keep practicing. And you don't wait. As soon as you see someone doing something well, you acknowledge them. You try to make that a habit."

"I like that, thinking of it as a commitment." The dogs were straining at their leashes, trying to make us get home faster.

Caffey said, "Slow down, girls. You're going to choke yourselves. We're almost home." He said, "Giving any kind of acknowledgement is the place to start—even 'good job' is better than nothing—but giving an acknowledgement with added depth makes it more meaningful."

I didn't quite understand. "Added depth? Do you mean just elaborate?"

"That's a start. It helps if you're more specific than 'good job.' Exactly what did they do that was so great? Let them know you recognize it."

"I guess I could do that without it feeling fake."

"It might feel awkward but it has to be real. If it's not authentic it's going to be counterproductive. Once you've acknowledged the details of their accomplishment, you can add more depth by acknowledging what they went through in order to do this great job. You could also let them know what impact their work had on you—what it meant to you—and what impact you see their accomplishment having on the future of the company or their career."

I shook my head. "That sounds like an awful lot to

say every time."

"You don't say all of that every time. But when the accomplishment calls for it, this kind of meaningful acknowledgment can draw out the best in someone. When I've gotten an acknowledgment like that, it's inspired me. I'm ready to do everything I can to contribute to the company."

We stopped at the start of Caffey's long dirt driveway and let the dogs off the leashes. Caffey took off his hat. "Let's rest by the pool for a minute. The dogs like to cool off on the steps."

Caffey unlatched the pool gate, and the dogs, panting heavily, ran onto the pool's first step. They settled in the water up to their necks. Caffey and I took our shoes off and sat on the edge. We put our feet in the cold water.

I'd been thinking over what Caffey had said. "It must be an inspiring place to work if you have people throughout the company expressing that kind of appreciation."

"It is. It's great having people look to give acknowledgement anywhere they see a need for it, whether it's to someone below them, at their same level or even above them. For the first time in my working life, I've been acknowledged by people below me. When I get an acknowledgment like that, I want to be the best leader I can be."

I said, "If we don't count the acknowledgments you've given me, I can't remember the last time someone acknowledged me."

"We try not to have that happen at Pinnacle. If acknowledgment is missing, we're committed to giving the appropriate person a heads-up and asking them to give the needed acknowledgment."

I bobbed my feet in and out of the water. "I bet there were a lot of people at Halton that didn't get the appreciation they needed," I said. "I know I hardly acknowledged anyone that last year."

Caffey nodded. "That's true. And when they complained about it, I used to make excuses for you."

"It's no wonder I wasn't getting the best out of our people," I chided Caffey. "You weren't letting me know I needed to acknowledge them. What's with that?" I laughed a little.

"I didn't know back then that by making excuses instead of doing something to change the situation, I became part of the problem, too. I actually thought I was being a good guy."

We both laughed. "Yeah, some kind of good guy you were."

One of the dogs got out of the pool and shook herself dry. She pounced over onto a grass patch beside the pool deck and rolled around on her back.

I lay back on the deck with my feet and legs still in the pool. I watched the sky and reflected on our conversation. "It's strange. I don't usually feel comfortable when someone acknowledges me. The few times I can remember being acknowledged, I ended up saying, 'I was just doing my job. That's nothing. You should really be acknowledging so-and-so.' I feel like I want to deflect it. I don't know why I do that."

"I find myself doing that a lot, too. I've had to work on catching myself deflecting acknowledgment. If you push an acknowledgment off like that, you're letting someone who's reached out to you fall flat — like you're dismissing a gift someone's trying to give you. I've found the best thing to do is just say, 'Thank you.'"

I smiled. "In that case, if I didn't say it the other night, thank you."

Caffey chuckled, "You're welcome."

ACKNOWLEDGMENT AND APPRECIATION

Today...

On my drive back to the office, I walked through my mental checklist of people I wanted to acknowledge. One of my daily goals was to give at least one acknowledgment. I remembered Linda Gray and her work on the strategic plan. I'd been meaning to talk to her. I called her office on my cell phone.

"Linda? It's Barry. If you have a minute, I'd like to talk to you before the meeting... No, no. Don't worry. It's good. I just want to acknowledge you for the work you've done... All right, I'm pulling into the parking lot. I'll be right over."

On my way to her office I ran through the steps of a good acknowledgment in my head. I wanted to be specific about what she had done and what she had to go through to accomplish it. I was clear on that part. Next, I looked to see what impact her work had on the future of our company and me. After all the acknowledgments I'd given, I still felt a little awkward imagining how I was going to say it all. But I knew how important it could be to Linda and how vital it was to our company to have meaningful acknowledgments be a part of our culture.

Linda was on the computer when I got to her office. She pushed herself away from her desk and asked me to have a seat.

"Thanks for making time."

"Sure thing, Boss," she teased.

"I was thinking about what a contribution you've made to the development of this Zero Delay plan. You've been great about making sure to include people — figuring out who needed to be included, searching them out and getting their input. With the deadline we've been running on this plan, it's been hard for me to want to get more input. But it's essential to what we're doing. So, I acknowledge you for being a key person in keeping that alive in the process. It's taken a tremendous weight off me to know that I have someone who's making it happen. It means I don't have to be doing everything myself to keep us moving forward. So, thank you."

"Wow." She smiled. "Thank you. I'm kind of shocked by the personal visit, though. I thought I was just doing my job. But I really appreciate your acknowledgement."

"You did a great job, Linda."

Her smile got bigger. She couldn't contain a little laugh. "Thank you."

"And you took the acknowledgment really well, too. You tried to downplay it a little but not too much."

"It's hard not to, but I'm getting better."

"I know," I nodded. It was the same for me.

"It's funny that you came in here, because I was just thinking about how much Andy Marx has done for the project. Have you acknowledged him?"

I had to think for a minute. "A little."

"He needs to be acknowledged. My work on this plan would have been almost impossible without him. I used his first draft of the plan with so many people. Having it broken down into an easy-to-understand document made it so much easier to get people's input. And since he's a construction manager, I know there's no time at work for him to have gotten that draft done. He's obviously been putting in a lot of time on his own."

I hadn't thought about how much extra work he must have been putting into the project. "I should acknowledge him," I agreed. "You're right. I definitely will. I've said a few things to him, but it's been pretty casual. I'll make sure I acknowledge him in the meeting. In fact, that'd be a great way to start off. Thanks for the heads-up."

"You're welcome," she said.

I stood up. "By the way Linda, it would be useful if you acknowledged Andy, too, given what you just told me."

"I knew you were going to say that." She smiled again. "I'll do it before the day is over."

"Great. I'll see you in the meeting."

❖

I felt good walking back to my office. Giving an acknowledgment like that felt as good as receiving one. Both of us got a little inspiration from the exchange.

I saw Dave Shaver, one of our general superintendents, coming down the hallway towards me. I waved to him.

"Hey, Barry," he said. "Perfect. I wanted to talk to you before the meeting. I wanted to thank you and acknowledge you for how you've led us through this planning process. My guys, the other supers and foremen, really appreciate the chance they've had to shape Zero Delay. I know it's going to be a lot easier for them to get behind it now that they've had the chance to voice their ideas. The way you're leading this company is inspiring, Barry. I feel like we're making something together here, like we're all a part of it."

"Thanks, Dave." I felt genuinely appreciated. "Thanks

for saying that. It means a lot to me. It's funny. I was just acknowledging Linda for a very similar thing."

"I'm glad to hear it. And you're welcome." He clapped his hands. "OK, I'll see you in the meeting."

Having acknowledgments flowing through our company like this was energizing and inspiring all of us. It made Sonoran a fun place to work. And like Caffey had said, after Dave's acknowledgment I wanted to be an even better leader.

CHAPTER SIX

INCLUSION
AND
ALIGNMENT

A little over three years ago...

*L*ying on my back on the pool deck with my feet in the cool water and a little breeze blowing over me, I felt sleepy. I knew we had a little more to go, so I sat up, took my feet out of the water and sat cross-legged.

Caffey asked me, "Do you remember that plan you came up with a little before you sold the company—the plan that was going to give Halton 'a new future'?"

I winced. "I remember it. I remember telling you a barrel of monkeys should have been able to pull that one off. The way I had to try to force people to implement it was kind of the straw that broke the camel's back."

"I remember what a disappointment that was for you. You came up with a great plan. But as you saw, great plans by themselves aren't enough. When you don't practice what we call 'Inclusion,' it makes it more difficult to get people's buy-in. You have to push through a lot of resistance. You also don't get people's best work if you don't include them in the creation and design side of things."

I flicked away an ant that was searching the pool deck by my toes. "But things just drag on and on when you start bringing in a lot of other people. Especially when it's something as big as a company-wide plan."

"You're right," Caffey said. "If you try to include too many people, nothing gets done. But when you don't include the people that need to be included, you kill off your team. You miss out on the contribution other team members could make. You miss out on their excitement to put something into place that they were a part of making happen.

"The apparent slowdown of spending extra time to include people is deceptive. Again, like Roy says, 'You have to slow down to go faster.' You wasted so much more time trying to force people to get on board with your plan. You don't get anywhere near as much resistance when you do a good job of Inclusion."

I looked up at a passing cloud and felt overburdened. "It seems like I need to change the way I'm doing everything."

Caffey shook his head. "Don't make yourself wrong for the way you've been doing things. That's not the point of this. It's simple. Don't make it mean a lot. What you've been doing isn't working anymore, so you do something different to get what you want. You wanted 'Alignment' behind your plan. You wanted everyone focused behind the decision you made — all the key players owning it and championing it. But to get that kind of support, you have to include people up front. You have to practice Listening Generously, Speaking Straight, Being For Each Other and Acknowledgement and Appreciation when you ask for people's Alignment. It takes all those commitments for people to be able to authentically align behind something, especially when the decision's not their preference."

I still felt discouraged. "But when I look at where Sonoran is right now, it seems like an impossible journey to reach the place you're describing."

Caffey pulled his feet out of the water and turned towards me. "You don't have to be perfect at it to have it work. Everything we've talked about — the five commitments, Inclusion and Alignment — they're all cradled in a Context of Learning in that diagram I drew. You're always learning as you practice. No one's ever going to be the master of all this. You just start wherever you're at."

His family drove up the crunchy gravel driveway and the dogs jumped up barking. We let them out the gate and walked over carrying our shoes. Caffey's kids had gotten big. I told them how little I remembered them being. They smiled politely like they'd heard that a lot. I remembered what Caffey had told me about his daughter. "So, your dad's a good listener now that he's doing this Collaborative Way thing?"

"Yeah," she grinned. "He doesn't freak out about what I say as much any more. Or if he does, it's not for very long."

Caffey put his arm around her. "I have a good coach. She doesn't let me get away with anything less than good listening."

She smiled. "Yeah, I get to be the boss. I get to catch him when he messes up."

Caffey said, "I like not being the boss."

Diane invited me to stay for dinner, but I told her my wife was expecting me back in Tucson and I didn't want to take up anymore of Caffey's day. "I have some work to do tomorrow, too." I told them all how nice it was to see them again and said goodbye. I petted the dogs and thanked them for their company. Diane and the kids waved goodbye and they all went inside.

I sat on the hood of my car and put my shoes on. "I really want to thank you for spending your whole day beating the crap out of me with all this stuff." We both laughed. "No, really. Thanks for caring enough to try to help out."

"I'm glad I could. Thanks for being willing to listen. I know it's not all easy to hear."

I shook my head. "No, but I appreciate the challenge. I feel like you really opened my eyes today. I've come to see a lot of new things about my leadership, and I feel like I can do something positive about it now. I can see how these tools you showed me can help me make a difference at Sonoran. You did a great job of explaining it to me, too. Have you done this before?"

"Not exactly like this. I have co-led Collaborative Way trainings at Pinnacle, though. All the leaders in the company do. And in the normal course of business, everybody in the company coaches each other in the practice."

I looked at my old colleague with new respect. "I'm really thankful we ran into each other, Caffey. I'm going to make sure we don't go another five years without seeing each other."

"That was too long," he agreed.

We said goodbye, and I drove to the highway with the windows down. I put my arm out the window and surfed my hand through the currents of the cool wind. I felt hopeful as I sped down the on-ramp.

As I drove back to Tucson, I decided I was going to bring The Collaborative Way to Sonoran. For the first time in a long while, I was excited about our future.

Today...

I was walking away still beaming from Dave Shaver's acknowledgment when I heard him call my name. "I almost forgot," he said as he walked back towards me. "There's a great story I meant to tell you. It's about some of my foremen and crews working on the Camino Seco development." I stopped and turned to listen as he went on. "As you know, that site's a mess. We had one crew working with tough rock, another working in mud and another crew working on the street edge property, dealing with traffic. All the guys on the crews, including the foremen, were whining and moaning about the conditions and making all kinds of excuses for the delays. I found myself complaining to Jacob Brown about all of them being a bunch of whiners."

I hoped Jacob had called Dave out on his gossiping. "Did he let you get away with it?"

Dave laughed. "No, not at all. He was great about it. He said he's come to see that kind of bellyaching as a warning sign that he needed to practice Inclusion. He told me to try including the crews in the whole scope of the project and to share why I needed them to work through the tough conditions. So, I took his advice. I called a meeting and brought them all into the trailer. It was a tight fit in there. I explained why we needed them working where they were and why the timeline we had was important. After they understood the bigger picture, it was amazing. Within a day—well, actually, immediately—the whole character changed. People started coming up with ideas and making suggestions. This amazing shift had taken place. I hadn't appreciated the power of including people until I had such an obvious example play out for me. Now I can really see that when we leave people in the dark, it's only natural for them to complain, not give their all and do stupid things. In the past it always looked like they were just being petty jerks, but now I see that I wasn't including them. It wasn't just them."

I was delighted—not just that a difficult worksite had turned around but also at how The Collaborative Way had spread through our company. "That's one of the biggest lessons I've learned," I told him. "It almost took me two homebuilding companies to learn it. It's more powerful to work from the perspective of teamwork than 'Trust me; I know what I'm doing; just do what I ask.' It's done tremendous things for my leadership. That's a great story. You should tell it around the company. Stories of wins like that help keep The Collaborative Way vital."

"I will." He clapped his hands again. "OK, this time's for real. I'll see you in the meeting."

❖

Mike Bunt, the vice president of operations and head of the leadership team, knocked on my office door and let himself in. "We've got about fifteen minutes," he said.

I gathered together my folder, and we headed down the hallway. I stopped for my ritual sip from the water fountain.

I wiped the water from my mouth. "Let's go over

our focus."

Mike said, "OK. We're not here to make a decision. That's been done and that needs to be made clear with the team right up front. We're here to build Alignment. We're here to give people a chance to bring up and work out any concerns they have, any second thoughts. We want everyone to work them out in the room and not wait until they get out in the field. You're going to have to listen to them, Barry, be curious, set aside your filters and try to learn where they're coming from."

I knew exactly what he meant. "I had a great interaction with Frank today. It was a perfect example. Once I really listened to his concerns, we worked through them easily, and the whole conflict dissolved."

"That's what we want in the meeting," Mike said. We turned down the hallway to the meeting room. "Be clear with everyone that our goal for this meeting is for all of them to walk out of the room champions of Zero Delay. We're here to clear up anything that's in the way of them being a champion for it."

We stopped at the door. "All right," I said. "Let's go." We stepped inside the room, and I sat down at the head of the table. I thanked everyone for being there. "This is an important day in our company's history, and we have reason to be excited. I know I am. I know a lot of people in this room have put a lot of work into getting this initiative together. I want to take a moment to publicly acknowledge some of them. I'd like to acknowledge Andy for taking all this work we've put into Zero Delay and breaking it down into an easy-to-understand document. It's a hell of a feat …"

THE
EPILOGUE

Today...

I turned out of the office parking lot and let out a whoop. The meeting had gone better than I could have hoped. I had set the tone with my acknowledgment of Andy, and an inspired mood had carried on from there. There was some disagreement on a few points, and we had to work with a couple of people to get past points they were stuck on, but we did it. And now we had a plan well on its way to having company-wide support. I knew if we worked together to implement this plan, it would bring us to a whole new level of home construction. We were going to operate better than any other homebuilder in the country. I was proud of how we had used The Collaborative Way to become a powerful team. I was proud of the leader I had become.

I called my wife on the phone and told her to get ready. "Helen, we need the best food on earth tonight," I said. "We're driving to Phoenix."

I hadn't been to The Lincoln Ranch Grill since that night a little over three years ago when I'd run into Caffey. I hoped they still had that roasted duck and my favorite wine, the Pinot you couldn't get anywhere else. I was feeling appreciative. Out loud, I said, "Thank you, Carl Jung. Thank you to my favorite restaurant in Phoenix. Thank you to Caffey. And thank you to The Collaborative Way."

Acknowledgments

We are grateful for the overwhelming support and collaboration we received in writing this book. We extend our thanks and appreciation to everyone who contributed. We would like to individually thank a few of those who contributed so generously...

- ❖ Our respective wives, Lynne and Laura, for their love, support and tolerance throughout this project.
- ❖ The participants in American Infrastructure's 2005–06 Leadership Intensive for including Jason in their retreat and giving him a chance to experience The Collaborative Way® in action.
- ❖ Ross Myers, CEO of American Infrastructure, for his continual support and generosity.
- ❖ All the companies practicing The Collaborative Way® for providing inspiration and stories, some of which found their way into the book.
- ❖ Bill and Don Budinger, who were the first to take on the practice of The Collaborative Way® in their company, Rodel Products, Inc.
- ❖ Our colleague Jason Gore, whose rigorous input was instrumental in bringing the book to its final form.
- ❖ All the people who read the early versions of the book and provided insights and contributions, in particular: Steve Chandler, Mike Diccicco, Joy Fickett, Reesa Fickett, Larry Friedman, Sheryl Gurrentz, Steve Hardison, Bob Herbein, and Richard Peterson.

About the Authors

Jason Fickett lives in South Bend, Indiana with his wife and two children. He graduated summa cum laude from Arizona State University with a B.A. in English. His honors thesis was a collection of short stories. In addition to writing fiction, he has co-authored and edited several non-fiction works. He can be reached by e-mail at jasonfickett@gmail.com.

❖

Lloyd Fickett founded the management consulting firm Lloyd Fickett and Associates, Inc., in 1983. He developed The Collaborative Way® while consulting privately-owned companies through rapid growth, mergers, acquisitions, competitive challenges and other market pressures. For the last decade he has helped companies use The Collaborative Way® to build the futures they envision.

You can further explore this designed and intentional way of working together at www.collaborativeway.com. Lloyd can be reached by e-mail at lloyd@collaborativeway.com or at 303-499-0766.

The Collaborative Way®

We all come to the workplace with different backgrounds and expectations about how we're supposed to work together. As a result we are prone to ineffectiveness, misunderstanding and upset. In order to create an environment conducive to collaboration, we need to design and take on learning an intentional way of working together. The Collaborative Way® is one such model. It is a simple model that provides mutual understanding and a common language, which produces a powerful structure for ongoing coaching and learning. For well over a decade, it has proven its ability to provide a critical strategic advantage and satisfying workplace.

For more information or to join our free newsletter, visit our website at www.collaborativeway.com.

❖

To order additional copies of:

THE COLLABORATIVE WAY

*A Story About Engaging the
Mind and Spirit of a Company*

visit our website at www.collaborativeway.com